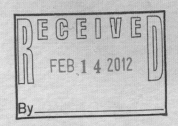

For my father, George Franklin,
a natural leader,
and for my mother, Mary Margaret,
who never forgets a birthday
—M.M.

For Joe Goldstein,
my grandpa the artist
—B.B.

Text copyright © 2012 by Margaret McNamara
Cover art and interior illustrations copyright © 2012 by Barry Blitt

Schwartz & Wade Books and the colophon are trademarks of Random House, Inc.

Visit us on the Web! randomhouse.com/kids

Educators and librarians, for a variety of teaching tools, visit us at randomhouse.com/teachers

*Library of Congress Cataloging-in-Publication Data*
McNamara, Margaret.
George Washington's birthday / Margaret McNamara ; illustrations by Barry Blitt.—1st ed.
p. cm.
Summary: On George Washington's seventh birthday, he does chores, misbehaves, and dreams of a day
when his birthday will be celebrated by all.
ISBN 978-0-375-84499-7 (trade) — ISBN 978-0-375-94458-1 (glb)
1. Washington, George, 1732–1799—Childhood and youth—Juvenile fiction. [1. Washington, George, 1732–1799—Childhood and youth—Fiction.
2. Birthdays—Fiction.] I. Blitt, Barry, ill. II. Title.
PZ7.M47879343Ge 2012
[E]—dc22
2010051259

The text of this book is set in Celestia Antiqua.
The illustrations were rendered in watercolor.
Book design by Rachael Cole

MANUFACTURED IN CHINA
10 9 8 7 6 5 4 3 2 1
First Edition

# George Washington's Birthday

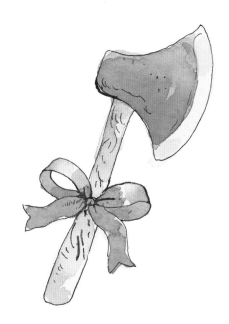

## A Mostly True Tale

WRITTEN BY

### Margaret McNamara

•

ILLUSTRATED BY

### Barry Blitt

schwartz & wade books · new york

When George Washington went to sleep Friday night, he was six years old.

When he woke up on Saturday, he was seven.

*It's my birthday*, he thought. *Happy birthday to me.*

George went down to breakfast. He peered out the kitchen door and checked the temperature.

"Another cold day," he said to his mother. "But I guess there's nothing *special* about that."

"Certainly not," she said. "Now eat your porridge and mind the baby."

After breakfast, George went to the library for his morning lessons.

"Get to work, George," said his half brother Augustine.

"I *am* working," said George.

"And don't blot your copybook!"

"Tyrant," muttered George, under his breath.

George was usually very good at arithmetic. But not this morning.

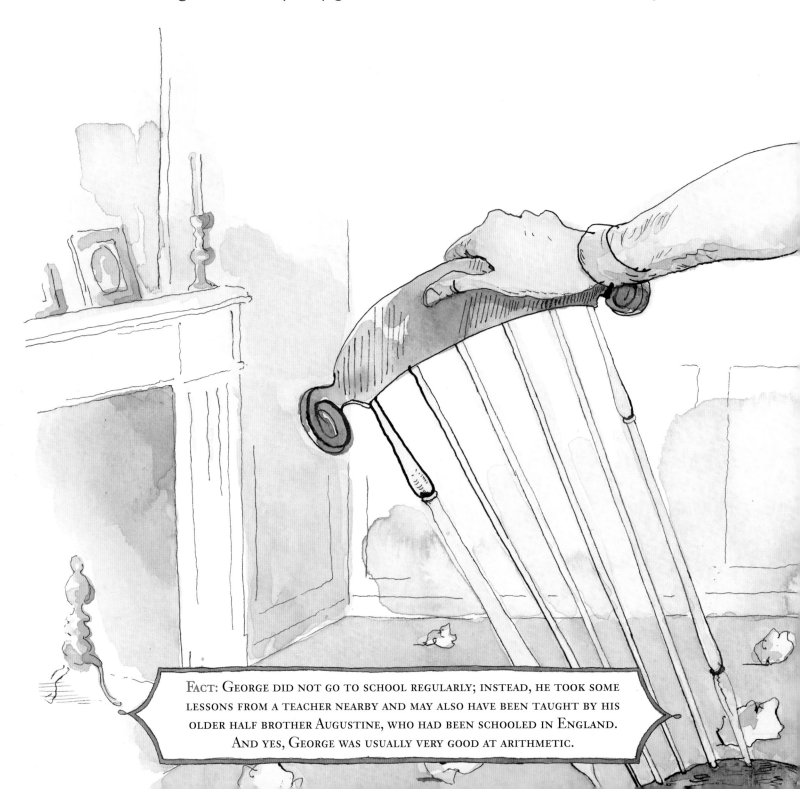

FACT: GEORGE DID NOT GO TO SCHOOL REGULARLY; INSTEAD, HE TOOK SOME
LESSONS FROM A TEACHER NEARBY AND MAY ALSO HAVE BEEN TAUGHT BY HIS
OLDER HALF BROTHER AUGUSTINE, WHO HAD BEEN SCHOOLED IN ENGLAND.
AND YES, GEORGE WAS USUALLY VERY GOOD AT ARITHMETIC.

Augustine marked his paper.

"All wrong," he said with a sigh. "You'll never amount to anything."

"Someday I'll be the boss of you," said George, but he made sure his brother couldn't hear.

George gave up on his lessons and went outside to visit the horses.

He patted his father's old dray. She snorted at him.

"When I'm older, I'll ride a horse even bigger than you," said George.

He imagined what he would name his own horse when he got older.

Then George noticed how cold it was. *I bet I'm turning blue*, he thought.

FACT:
GEORGE WAS
OVER SIX FEET TALL
WHEN HE GREW UP,
AND HE RODE VERY
TALL HORSES, TOO.
ONE OF HIS FAVORITE
HORSES WAS CALLED
BLUESKIN.

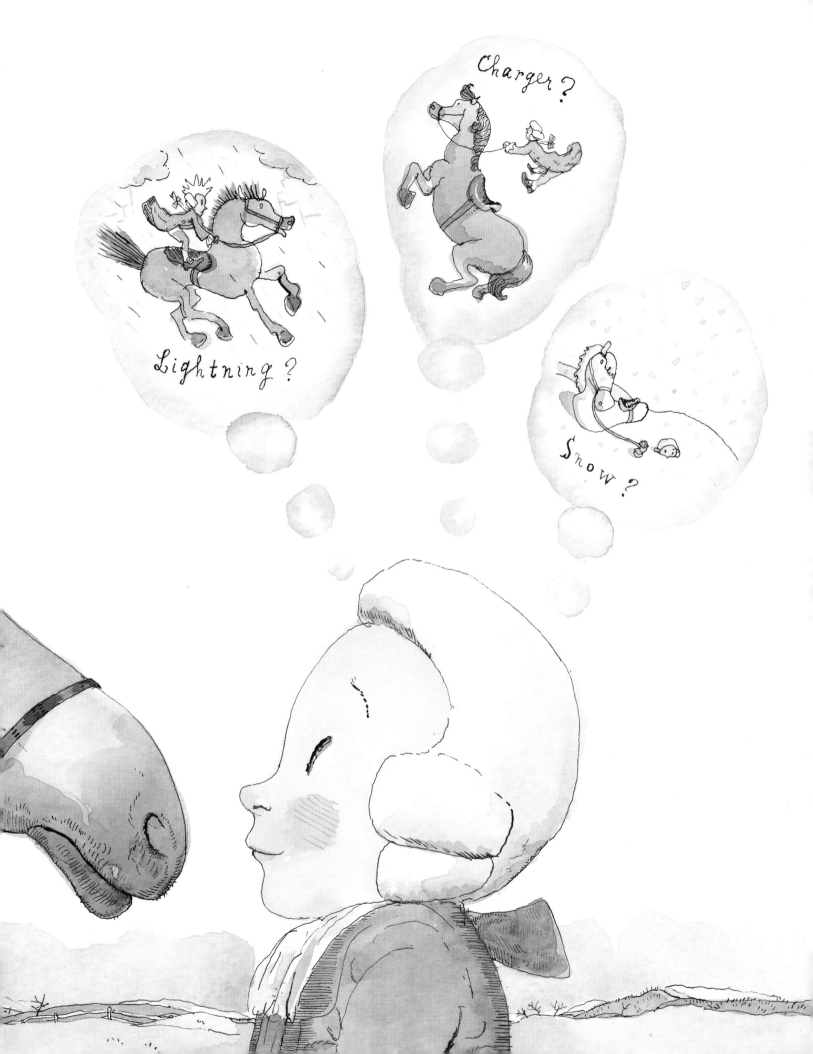

To warm himself up, George started tossing stones into the river. "Some birthday"—*toss*—"this is," George said.

A friend of his brother's strode by. "Bet you can't throw one of those all the way across the river," said the young man.

"Bet I can," said George. He screwed up his eyes and made a birthday wish. Then he leaned back, wound up, and threw the stone all the way to the other side of the Rappahannock River.

"Lordy! That's pretty good for a six-year-old," said the young man. And he ran off.

George was so peeved at being called a six-year-old that he tried to toss another stone across the river.

It sank before it got halfway over.

By the time he got home, George was cold and
grumpy and ready for some sweet tea by the fire.
He waved to his father, working in the orchard.

"Glad to see you, son," said George's father.
"You can help me prune these cherry trees."

"But, Papa—" George began.

"Fetch a hatchet," said his father.

George fetched a hatchet. He hacked off old tree branches. It was hard work. His hand ached. His back was sore. *This is no way to spend a birthday,* thought George. *I'm so mad I could just—*

George's father strode over to his son. "Who did this?" he asked, though George thought the answer must be pretty obvious.

"Don't you know what day it is?" asked George.

"It's Saturday," said his father. "And I'd advise that you think before you speak again."

George figured he'd better confess.

"Father," said George at last, "I cannot tell a lie. It was I who chopped down the tree." George always used his best grammar when he was in trouble.

His father sighed. "I'm glad you told the truth, son," he said.

George started to smile.

"But I am not happy about this tree." George stopped smiling.

"I suppose you'd better chop it up now that the damage is done,"
his father said, "and put it in the woodshed to dry."

The woodshed was across a little creek from the cherry orchard. Back and forth George carried the heavy loads of wood, crossing the icy creek each time. "Hope I never have to do this again," he said to himself.

**FACT:** IN ONE OF THE MOST IMPORTANT BATTLES OF THE REVOLUTIONARY WAR, GEORGE HAD TO CROSS THE DELAWARE RIVER MANY TIMES, IN BOATS CARRYING VERY HEAVY LOADS, IN ORDER TO DEFEAT THE BRITISH.

At last he finished his work.

"Now clean your face and hands and powder your wig and occupy yourself gainfully until dinnertime," said his father.

MYTH: MANY PEOPLE BELIEVE THAT GEORGE WASHINGTON WORE A WIG, BUT HE DID NOT. WHEN HE GOT OLDER HE POWDERED HIS WHITE HAIR TO MAKE HIMSELF LOOK MORE DISTINGUISHED.

THE New-England Courant.

Cherry Tree Mystery Solved.

R

Don't Axe
Don't Tell
Repealed

George went to his room. He got out a piece of paper and started writing.

But George wasn't sure this was what his father would call gainful occupation.

Be it known that in good time, my birthday will be hailed and celebrated at a grand and elegant dinner attended by multitudes and

FACT: ALMOST A HUNDRED YEARS AFTER GEORGE TURNED SEVEN, HIS BIRTHDAY WAS COMMEMORATED BY HIS FRIEND GENERAL LAFAYETTE AT A GRAND AND ELEGANT DINNER IN WASHINGTON, DC.

So he thought and he thought, and he came up with some other ideas, ideas he believed his father would like.

Think before you Speak. When you Sit down, Keep your Feet firm and Even, Keep your Nails clean and Short. If You Cough, Sneeze, Sigh, or Yawn, do it not Loud.

FACT: GEORGE REALLY DID WRITE A LIST HE CALLED "110 RULES OF CIVILITY AND DECENT BEHAVIOR," AND THESE ARE SOME OF HIS ACTUAL RULES. HE CARRIED THE LIST AROUND WITH HIM TO HELP HIM REMEMBER HOW TO BE A GENTLEMAN. HE PROBABLY DID NOT START WRITING THE RULES WHEN HE WAS SEVEN YEARS OLD, BUT BY THE AGE OF SIXTEEN HE HAD WRITTEN THEM ALL.

He worked so hard on his list that he did not hear the bell for dinner. "George!" called his mother. "Get down here at once."

George hurried down the stairs.

When he opened the door to the dining room, he got a mighty surprise.

"Happy birthday, George!"
said his family.

The family sat down to dinner and had a grand feast in
honor of the birthday boy.

FACT:
THE WASHINGTONS WOULD
NOT HAVE THROWN A PARTY FOR
GEORGE, BUT THEY MIGHT HAVE
HAD A LARGE FAMILY DINNER ON
HIS BIRTHDAY.

"I thought you had all forgotten," said George.

His mother gave him a squeeze. "How could anyone forget your birthday, George Washington?" she said.

"Oh, Mama," said George. "You only say that because you're my mother."

But to tell the truth, nobody did forget George Washington's birthday ever again.

# GEORGE WASHINGTON TELLS THE TRUTH

The story you just read is fiction—that means it was made up. But there is a lot that's true in this story. So I'm going to set the facts straight.

When I was seven, I lived on the banks of the Rappahannock River in Virginia. I had two half brothers, Lawrence and Augustine; a younger sister, Betty; and three younger brothers, Samuel, John, and baby Charles. You don't see Lawrence in the story because he was living in England at the time.

It's true I was a serious little boy. I was very interested in the weather, and in the landscape around our house, and in my lessons, of course. I really did write out 110 rules to live by, and I kept them with me as I grew older. I rode horses almost all my life, and they did have the names Charger, Lightning, Snow, and Blueskin. I commanded the American soldiers as they traveled by ferry back and forth across a river. I was a general in the Revolutionary War, and I became the first president of the United States. But when I was seven years old I didn't know that any of that would happen!

I got to be such an important leader that lots of myths grew up about me. Teachers and parents used me as an example of how *really* good children should behave. The story about how I threw a rock or a silver dollar across a river was told to show how strong I was. (I was strong, but not *that* strong!)

In 1800, a preacher named Mason Locke Weems wrote a book called *The Life of George Washington*. Parson Weems made up the story about the cherry tree for his book, to show my goodness and virtue.

It's funny to think that a story about the truth was actually not true!

Nowadays, my birthday is a holiday called Presidents' Day. Banks, post offices, and schools are closed on the third Monday of February to celebrate. But when I was born, it was just a cold February day. In fact, we used a different calendar back then, so according to that calendar, I was born on February 11, 1732. Then we changed our calendar (it was very confusing!) and my birthday moved to February 22, 1732. I suppose my mama was right—nobody forgets my birthday anymore!